Thumbelina

A Tale about Being Nice

Retold by Catherine Lukas
Illustrated by Beverly Branch

Famous Fables™

Reader's Digest Young Families

Long ago, a woman visited a good fairy because she wanted very much to have a child.

"Plant this barley seed in a flowerpot," advised the fairy. "Watch closely as it grows."

The fairy's instructions were odd, but the woman trusted the fairy and did as she was told. A large flower blossomed. Inside was a very tiny girl.

"Gracious me!" said the woman to the girl. "You are only as big as my thumb. I will call you Thumbelina!"

The woman gave Thumbelina a polished walnut shell for a bed and lined it with soft rose petals.

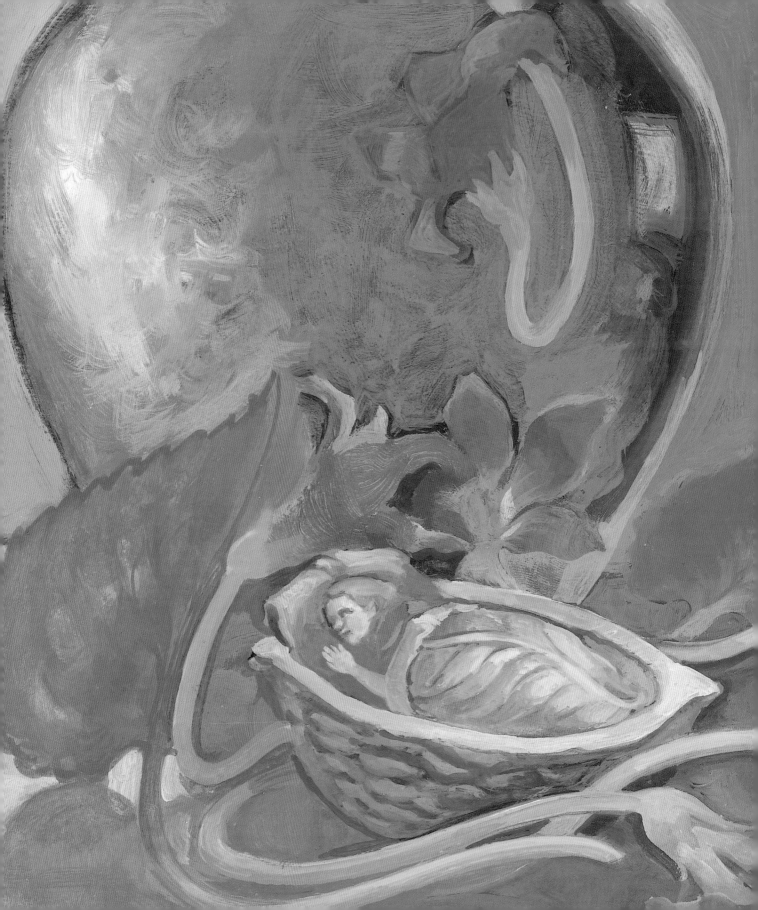

One night, a large toad peeped through an open window and saw Thumbelina sleeping.

"This girl would make a beautiful wife for my son!" thought the toad. So the toad hopped into the room, picked up the walnut shell, and carried it carefully to a large lily pad in the middle of a stream.

When Thumbelina awoke the next morning, she could see it was impossible for her to reach land. She cried and cried. Soon the large toad, along with a smaller one, appeared. The large toad said, "Here is my son. He will be your husband." This dreadful news made Thumbelina cry even harder.

Some fish who were nearby in the stream overheard the toad. They felt so sorry for Thumbelina that they tried to help her. Quietly the fish chewed through the stem of the lily pad until it floated freely.

The lily pad began to float downstream, with
Thumbelina on top. A beautiful butterfly fluttered by.
Thumbelina gave one end of her sash to the butterfly,
who used it to steer the lily pad. The girl and the
butterfly drifted far from the toads' reach.

Just when Thumbelina thought she was safe,
a large winged beetle flew by and snatched her up.
He took her to a tree, where he fed her some honey
to calm her.

"You are quite beautiful," he said.

The female beetles were jealous of Thumbelina's beauty. They did not want the girl to stay. So they said to the male beetle, "Poor thing, she has only two legs and no wings. It would be hard for her to live with us."

"What they say is true," thought the male beetle. "I will set the little girl free."

As they flew through the forest, the beetle asked Thumbelina where she would like to go. She pointed to a daisy patch. The beetle set her down and flew off.

Thumbelina wove a bed out of leaves and sipped nectar from the flowers. She loved listening to the birds sing. And so summer and autumn passed. When winter arrived, the sweet-singing birds flew to warmer places. The flowers shriveled up. Cold and hungry, Thumbelina wandered through the woods. At last, she saw a mouse's den in an old cornfield. Thumbelina knocked on the door.

"You poor little thing," said the mouse when she saw the girl shivering. "You must come in."

The mouse said Thumbelina could stay for the winter if she would keep the den clean. Grateful to be in such a warm and safe place, Thumbelina agreed.

One day the mouse said, "My neighbor, the mole, is joining us for tea. He is quite rich and would make a wonderful husband for you."

But when Thumbelina met the mole, she knew she did not want him for a husband. Although he was rich and wore a beautiful velvet coat, he lived underground and did not like the sun or the flowers.

After tea, the mole led Thumbelina through a tunnel to see his home. On the way, the mole pointed to a bird he thought was dead lying on the ground.

Thumbelina recognized the bird. He had sung to her in the summer. She put her head on his chest. *Thump! Thump!* The swallow's heart was beating. He was alive!

Each day, Thumbelina brought water for the swallow to drink. Slowly he grew strong enough to fly.

"Will you fly away with me?" asked the swallow.

"I cannot leave the kind mouse," replied the girl.

"Farewell, then, and thank you," he said.

When Thumbelina returned to the den, the mouse told her, "The mole wants to marry you!"

"I cannot marry the mole!" cried Thumbelina. "I cannot live without sunshine."

"You should be thankful for your good fortune," said the mouse. "I've already hired three spiders to make your wedding dress."

The day before the wedding, Thumbelina went outside to say farewell to the sun. A bird was singing. Thumbelina knew it was the swallow she had nursed back to health. She told him about her marriage to the mole the next day.

The swallow asked her again to fly away with him. This time, Thumbelina agreed. She sat on the swallow's back, and the two flew over forest and sea.

After a long journey, the swallow and Thumbelina arrived in a beautiful, warm land. There was a palace of white marble. At the top of it were many nests. One nest was the swallow's home.

"My nest is too high for you to live in," the swallow said. "I will put you on a flower below. There you will be happy."

Inside the flower, Thumbelina and the swallow found a tiny man! They were very surprised. The man wore a gold crown and had delicate wings. He was the king of the flowers!

Thumbelina told the king all about her adventures, and how she and the swallow had helped each other.

The king was touched by the maiden's kind and caring heart and fell in love with her. "Will you marry me and become queen of the flowers?" he asked.

"Yes, I will," replied Thumbelina.

All at once, the other flowers opened. In each was a little lord and lady with a present for Thumbelina. One gift was a pair of wings. Now Thumbelina could fly, too.

The swallow sang at the wedding. Never before had a bird sung so beautifully. In his song, the swallow told the story of the little lost maiden who had shown him great kindness and had finally found a home.

Famous Fables, Lasting Virtues
Tips for Parents

Now that you've read Thumbelina, *use these pages as a guide to teach your child the virtues in the story. By talking about the story and its message and engaging in the suggested activities, you can help your child develop good judgment and a strong moral character.*

About Being Nice

Learning to be a good, kind person is the foundation for developing many important virtues, including respect for others, sharing, empathy, and honesty. It is never too early to start teaching children the meaning of "Do unto others as you would have others do unto you." But as every parent knows, we usually need to spell out exactly what we mean when we tell our children to "be nice." Teaching your child good manners, to share toys, and to do family chores will help your child learn to live by the Golden Rule.

1. *Teach good manners.* Learning to say "please" and "thank you" is age-appropriate even for very young children. Reminded often enough, children will eventually internalize the correct usage of these simple words. Older children can learn to shake someone's hand and to say, "How do you do?" while making eye contact. Be sure to praise your children lavishly when they use good manners.

2. *Be a model.* Young children copy the behavior of their parents and older siblings. If you use good manners and treat others with courtesy and respect, your child will learn to do the same. In turn, show that you respect your child by listening to what he says. Parents who listen to their children are teaching them that words have power and that using words can be more effective than throwing tantrums or being physical.

3. *Assign home chores.* Even very young children can help with chores, such as setting and clearing the table, matching socks, and distributing clean laundry. Although it's often easier to do many of these tasks ourselves, it's important to help children understand that the needs of the family must be balanced with their own needs.